Clint Faraday Mysteries
#13
The Body In the Bay

The body of a woman in snorkeling gear is found in the bay. She was entangled in mangrove roots. There was no reason anyone would snorkel there – plus she could easily have gotten out of those roots.

What really happened? Why was she there? What happened to the two men who were with her when they left Almirante?

Clint Faraday Mysteries
#13
The Body In the Bay

Contents

About the author

CD was born in Lakeland, Florida. His education is in genetics and botany. He has traveled over much of the world, particularly when he was in music as a rock rhythm guitarist with some well-known bands in the late sixties and early seventies. He has worked as a high steel worker and as a longshoreman, clerk, orchidist, bar owner, salvage yard manager and landscaper – among other things.

CD began writing fiction in 1984 and has more than 115 books published as of this time in SciFi, murder, orchid culture and various other fields.

He now resides in Bocas del Toro and David, Panamá, where he continues research into epiphytic plants. He loves the culture of the indigenous people and counts a majority of his closer friends among that group. Several have "adopted" him as their father. He funds those he can afford through the universities where they have all excelled. "The Indios are very intelligent people, they are simply too poor (in material things and money. Culturally, they are very wealthy) to pursue higher education."

CD loves Panamá and the people. He plans to spend the rest of his life in the paradise that is Panamá

- Estrelita Suarez V.

CD is involved in research of natural cancer cure at this time. It has proven effective in all cases, so far. It is based on a plant that has been in use for thousands of years, is safe, available, and cheap. He has studied botany, and was cured of a serious lymphoma with use of the plant, *Ambrosia peruviana.*

Information about this cure is free on the FaceBook page, Ambrosia peruviana for cancer. CD asks only that all who try it please report on its effectiveness on that group.

A Typical Day

Clint Faraday, retired PI from Florida, brought his boat into his deck. He and Judi Lum, the attractive Taiwanese nextdoor neighbor, climbed out and tied the boat. Clint handed her the gear and smaller items, then he put the chest of fish on the deck, followed by the other paraphernalia they took on their fishing jaunts.

"It was nice all day, today," Judi said. "We got enough for both our freezers and a few for Ben. It was too bad he couldn't come."

Ben was Ben Longstreet, a neighbor. He was gay, which was a big "So what?" in Bocas del Toro, Panamá.

Silvio Lopez, an Indio friend, came by in his cayuca and greeted them, "Coin dere!" They returned the greeting. Both of them spoke some of the Ngobe language (Ngobere). Clint was becoming fluent. Most of his closer friends were Indios.

Judi brought a deep pan from the kitchen and sorted the fish. She left two large ones in the chest and told Clint she'd borrowed the chest from Ben, so he could carry it back with the fish.

Clint grinned and helped her take her gear and fish home, then returned and cleaned the fish. He put Ben's in the ice and carried the chest to Ben's house. Earl, his newest love, took the fish inside. He said Ben would be home from work in half an hour. He'd cook up one of the fish for dinner. He was a gourmet chef, so the meal would be between great and fantastic.

"They're big. I'll expect you and Jude around six thirtyish. No excuses. I have a good almondine sauce I make, old-fashioned hush-puppies, garden salad, and mustard greens from Volcan. We were in Cerro Punta last week, so I brought a lot of them back. They're a weed up there. Nobody eats them. I cooked up enough for a month or two and froze them for your freezer. I know you like them as much as we do. There's nothing better with fish."

Clint said he'd be there. He called Judi. She said that would be perfect. She was planning to cook fish, herself, but she couldn't hope to compete with Earl in the cooking area.

Clint went back home to check out his comp and calls, answered a few e-mails, deleted twenty some-odd spam messages, then cleaned up to lay around until a few minutes after six. He took a bottle of good Chianti, called Judi to say, "Let's go!" and went to meet her at his gate and to walk the two blocks (if they'd had blocks there) to Ben's. They spent a pleasant evening there. They went home at about eleven. Judi decided to go to a friend's house, but Clint was tired. He sacked out.

In the morning, Clint went into town where he talked with the regulars at the Golden Grill, then to the market for a few things, then back to his house. He got a call from a friend at Punta Robalo and took his boat around to his place, about an hour and a half by boat. They solved the problem, a silly non-issue type of thing about who owned what. The Indios have no ownership, in that sense, in their culture. It was a misunderstanding that could have grown into something more, but probably wouldn't have.

Clint went back home at three o'clock. He was tying the boat to the dock when his celular buzzed. He answered, to find it was Sergio Sanchez, head of the police in Bocas Town. Some snorkelers had found a body in the bay. It looked like a woman had been snorkeling near the mangroves, had gotten entangled in the roots, and had drowned.

"Why tell me?" Clint asked.

"It just doesn't feel right. No one has been reported missing. She was a tourist, I think, so wouldn't have been there alone."

"Yeah. That smells – and I haven't even been out there yet. Where was it?"

"About a quarter of the way from the mainland to Dolfin Point. We brought the body in. There's nothing to see there."

"I'll come to the station in the morning."

"Anything new happened since you called?" Clint asked Sergio, in the morning.

"Except that there were no signs of violence on the body, more than would be natural for that kind of thing, no."

Clint didn't know where to go with no more information. "Who was she?"

"We don't know, yet. I'm having her prints identified. They'll have that from her passport, I hope. Nobody's been asking about a misper or anything."

"No ID of any type on the body?"

"A small tattoo on her left ankle. A fourleafed clover."

"Irish."

"Uh-huh."

"Well, I'll talk with Doc, then check around. Judi can find information faster than we can, a lot of the time, so I'll get her on it."

They discussed fishing a moment, then Clint headed for the Golden Grill. None of the regulars had heard anything about anyone going out and not coming back.

This wasn't getting anywhere. Clint went home. He asked Judi to ask around when she was in Bocas Town and elsewhere.

"I'm going to Changuinola with Ana and Yveth. Maybe they'll know something there."

There wasn't much to do. Clint decided to paint his fence. He would have to know more to decide if he even wanted to bother with it. It did intrigue him. It was a fairly obvious murder.

"... that there was a woman there with two men, sort of

reddish auburn hair and green eyes, good figure, maybe five six or so. They went somewhere. Nobody came back. Nilsa, at the hotel, said they were from Canada. They had Canadian passports. She gave me the numbers and names, James Besford, Charles Dennis, and Shannon O'Brien. I gave Serg the passport information. He said the woman fit the description. They were all staying in San Juan, Costa Rica, for a short while. O'Brien, for several months.

"That's about it for what I could find," Judi finished.

"Which was a heck of a lot more than Sergio or I could find in the time. It gives us a starting place, other than a body in the bay."

They chatted awhile about the strange people she ran across in Changuinola, then she went home to clean up for a dinner date. Clint cleaned up and walked into town to stop at the Toro Loco before going to El Ultimo Refugio for a good meal. He met a girl from Canada, they hit it off, she was on vacation to learn about life, she was not a virgin, but not very experienced, either.

Besford and Dennis were from Canada. She had stopped for two days in San Jose' Costa Rica. Clint managed to mention them in the way Judi taught him. She had met them once, in a bar, where she had talked with them about Canada. They were with some people by the name of Boucher, from France. There was some hood who came in and they left with him. That was all she knew.

It was a very good night. In the morning, after Eileen had gone to meet her traveling mates, Clint went to the police station to see what Sergio had learned. There was an alert out for the two men. They hadn't left the country, according to immigration. Their passports had not been used or stamped at exit. They were being checked in Canada, information from which would come in about eleven.

Clint said he would ask around about it. He had a lot of friends in that part of the archipelago who might have seen something. He went back, got his boat, and headed for Tierra Oscura, Isla Popa, Isla Pastore, Shark Hole, and the Crawl Cay end of Bastimentos. One Indio family, who were out between Dolfin Point and Isla Pastore, saw who might have been them. They had a white and green fiberglass boat, 16', with a 50 horse four stroke Yamaha. There was one woman with dark reddish hair with two men, one blond and one dark-haired. The dark man's hair was a little long. The blond might have had a pony tail. The men were in their early twenties or so and were tall and strong. The dark-haired one had a tattoo on his left shoulder of a tiger and, on the right, just a pattern in red, green and blue.

The Indios can give excellent descriptions if you know what – and how – to ask. This was a combination of the father, who noticed the woman, particularly, the mother, who noticed much about the men, and the three children in their early teens who noticed little points, here and there. The oldest son was gay. He noticed everything about the men. They were built like bodybuilders, but maybe a little bit slimmer. They were attractive, in a way. (The Indios take that as a matter of course, also.)

They passed about six meters away, just at the point. The boat was headed into the bay. The Indios were headed out around the point. The whole family worked the cocoa finca there. The mother said she thought she'd seen the boat before, on the mainland-facing side of Isla San Cristobal.

Clint went to the little marina on San Cristobal to learn that a woman named Shannon O'Brien had rented the boat for the day, two days ago. He had her passport number and so forth. It was the same as Sergio had. An Indio brought the boat back just before dark. He said the people in it paid him to bring it back because they had to hurry to get to the Panamá City bus that took on passengers in Almirante. The Indio was Daniel Santana, who Clint knew.

Clint went to Almirante, where he found Daniel, who said there were two surfer-type men in the boat. They said they had to get their bags and so forth from the Hotel San Francisco, then back to the station to get the bus. They couldn't depend on getting back in time, so they gave him ten dollars to take the boat back.

"What did they have in the boat? Surfboards or fishing tackle or what?"

"Just some snorkeling stuff and two box ice chests. The chests were heavy. Both the men were strong, but it took both of them to take the boxes from the boat. They put them in the back of one of the small-truck taxis, then went toward the hotel. I took the boat. I usually only get six dollars, so it was a good day!"

"Did you notice which taxi it was?"

"I think from Changuinola. It wasn't from here. I only saw it once or twice before. They had a lot of money. Hundred dollar bills. I told them I couldn't change a twenty, much less a hundred. They had a ten and gave it to me to take the boat back for them."

He didn't know anything else.

Now Clint was curious. A woman was dead and her two companions had gone off with two large boxes. Clint went to the bus terminal. The two didn't take a bus from there to anywhere. They didn't take the David bus, either. The passenger manager would have definitely noticed them. The boxes would have cost extra if they were that heavy.

So. They had a taxi from Changuinola waiting – or did they call one? Did they take a taxi to David or elsewhere?

That would be between eighty and a hundred dollars. They had a lot of hundred dollar bills. Clint was suspicious about those boxes. He had a sneaky suspicion they were packed with hundred dollar bills. There was a lot of drug money in cash around that was in transit for laundering. Had they found a couple of those boxes with millions in cash and one of them ended up dead, while the other two escaped with the money?

Whatever, this was definitely the kind of thing he liked to investigate.

He headed back to Bocas Town to report on what he'd found and what he suspected to Sergio. Sergio said they were watching four people who they suspected were involved in drugs, right there in town. Vincento Salares, Georgio Mendez, Samuel D'Alesandro, and Noko Itumi. Itumi was, of course, Japanese. Clint had seen them around.

Clint went back to his house to work with the computer to check on all the names he had, so far. Very little came up, except Itumi. He was in and out of trouble in Colombia and Mexico before he moved to Venezuela, where he stayed reasonably clean. His contacts and crimes were mostly petite. Vincente Salares had one conviction of carrying an illegal weapon, a switchblade with a twelve centimeter blade. He was fined and spent three days in jail in Santa Marta, Colombia. It was looking like a drug money case, more and more.

Clint went into town, but the four were out in a boat for the day. Enrique had taken them out. They were scuba diving the inner reefs. They went out two or three times a week to the same area. They said they were studying the fish on that kind of reef to write a book about them to sell to tourists who wanted to know about the different blah, blah, blah. Put that together with the rest. They had stashed some boxes of cash under a little reef in an area almost nobody visited. The Canadians visited. They found the money. They took it. The reason the boxes were so heavy was because they were weighted.

That fit, but why not dump the weights when they moved it? That didn't fit.

Maybe it did! Maybe the weights were worth more than the money was! Gold or silver bars.

So? Why was Shannon dead? If it had been the foursome, they would have made it obvious she was "executed" for screwing around with their crooked money. The two Canadians would be acting very differently than they were. They wouldn't be leaving a trail.

Clint went back to Almirante to ask about the taxi. No one knew much. It wasn't a local. Maybe Changuinola.

Clint took a bus to Changuinola. A couple of people had noted the truck. One said he saw the woman in it two times, and one of the men, the blond one, once. It wasn't a local taxi.

Clint had an idea. He went to the police station. They knew him and would cooperate. The taxi had been noted and checked because the driver made local pickups and was overcharging. The locals knew the legal fares, but the tourists, particularly gringos, didn't. Two locals made complaints. The driver was forced to return their money and was warned that he was breaking national law and would end his crooked ass in jail for thirty days the next complaint they received. They didn't receive any more.

Clint had the taxi number. He checked it on the computer.

Veraguas? That was a long way and on the Pacific side. Now there was a good reason for suspicion!

Bigshots sometimes rented a taxi to take them anywhere. The taxi would take the fare where they wanted to go for un-regulated prices. They charged a lot for such trips. They too often didn't find a return fare, and had to take short-hop fares all the way back. They didn't hang around a town hundreds of kilometers from their base. They got back as fast as they could.

That was one big question. It might give him a starting point for investigation, more than a little strange.

Clint decided to have Sergio put out a quiet information request about the movements of that taxi. It would be noted at any checkpoints along the way. They had plenty of time to go to Veraguas or anywhere else, but he could hope they were being careful not to be noticed – which generally meant they were noted everywhere. He then went to his house to check his e-mail and such, then took his boat out to the area where the body was found. It wasn't the kind of place where people often went diving. The water was deep there, but it was in a sort of cove that didn't flush well, so the bottom was mud, if deep, and there were just too many jellyfish in that kind of place. Some of them could give a painful and dangerous sting. There were no reefs in there. The reefs were outside of the cove and around the end of the peninsula. The mangroves there had plenty of roots hanging in the water, but they were generally not attached to anything below, because of the steep drop of the bank. If a person were to get tangled in them, he or she could easily get to the surface by simply pushing them aside.

Clint went out to the area of the coral reefs. The woman's body was found with her snorkeling paraphernalia in place. She wouldn't be in there unless she was looking for something specific. That could well mean the body was brought into the bay after she was killed. Doc said she died of drowning, which could have occurred anywhere.

He could use the working assumption that she and her friends were snorkeling around one of the small coral heads or along the reef around the end of the peninsula, found the money or whatever, were taking it out, and were discovered.

Crap! She wouldn't be the one killed. She would damned well show some signs of resistance. A stranger couldn't have done it. That meant her two friends. The fact they were at that spot had to mean something.

Okay. Hook on that unexplained taxi. They were here to find that money. It was probably put there by them some time ago. When the heat died down they came after it – which didn't work, either. They wouldn't have brought her along in that case.

This was the kind of puzzle Clint claimed to hate, but he actually liked the challenge.

He went back to Bocas Town. Judi had nosed around a bit. She found that Shannon O'Brien had come to Changuinola in the taxi to meet Besford and Dennis. Marta Lima, whose sister worked at the Estranjero Hotel in Changuinola, said the two men booked a room for her the day before she arrived. They had the taxi driver staying in the Pension Grande Vista. Marta had Susana check on that.

There was nobody like Judi Lum for getting information!

An interesting note: the taxi driver, a large black man they called Gordo, seemed to be far more in charge at times than the others, though Shannon was also sometimes in charge, it seemed.

Gordo, in a small-truck taxi from Santiago. That should make him easy enough to find!

Clint thought about it for a few minutes, then packed a few things and told Judi he was headed for Santiago. There were answers there to – something he had damned little of, at the moment. Nothing made any sense in this one. He took his boat to Chiriqui Grande and caught the bus to David, stayed the night at the Pension Costa Rica in David, then caught an early bus for Santiago.

Santiago is a rather sleepy town in an area that specializes in cattle ranching. It's hot, much of the year, and reminded Clint of south central Texas, though it tended to more greenery. He always stayed at the Bocas del Toro Hotel there. He frequented the bar and restaurant across the carretera. He knew a number of people in the area, so was able to find that Gordo was David (Gordo) Silverano. He had gone somewhere a week or so before and hadn't returned. He lived part of the time in Veraguas, where he had a house. Yes, he was often taking the Irish lady places. She was even staying at his apartment for several days before they left. The two surfer types weren't known there at all.

Shannon used the internet café by The Pyramid, where the bus station was. She spent a lot of time there.

Clint found where the apartment was and spoke with the landlady. She said Gordo was usually quiet, and wasn't ever any real trouble, except he had women there. That wasn't at issue if it was just one or two for long periods, but he had a different one every week, it seemed. He was sometimes too bossy around his women. They sometimes got loud.

Clint got the taxi registration number from her and went to the registro to make a computer check on it. Gordo had a few minor tickets, one only days ago at the Rambala checkpoint, for not having the left turn signal light working.

Big deal! Taxis almost never used anything but the horn, anyhow!

Clint checked with the police checkpoint at La Mina, in the mountains. The taxis are noted when they pass, though they are seldom stopped. Gordo had come in the direction of David, two days before. He had two passengers, but they weren't checked. There was no alert out for any gringos.

Clint called Jose', a friend who drove a taxi in David, and asked if he knew Gordo. He had met him a couple of times, but didn't think he was in David now. He hadn't been there in a month or so.

Clint called the more important checkpoint near Tole'. Gordo and friends had not passed there. They had an alert to note if he came through and to get ID from any passengers, but not to delay him unless new orders came through.

They came through La Mina, but didn't come through Tole'. That meant somewhere between.

Clint caught a bus to David. He got off in Chiriqui. Gordo and company hadn't stopped there. They hadn't been seen there.

Clint went to Gualaca. Gordo and passengers, three men, had come through. They had stayed an afternoon, then left. They asked about Boquete and points between.

Boquete. They didn't go there.

Calderas? No. Clint was going all over the place to no advantage, and was getting tired of spending his day in a bus. There was a nice fairly new Honda XL for sale at a very good price just outside of Gualaca. Clint swore he would never own another car, but it had become necessary. He had plenty of money in the bank from some jobs, more than he had any use for, so he sighed and bought the thing and insurance and such. He had a license for Panamá, so sighed and swore again. He soon headed toward the carretera from that end. He stopped in Dolega, Anastasia, and Concepcion – where he found they had stayed last night, then drove off toward

Panamá City about two hours ago. There were three. They stayed at the hotel about a mile toward David.

Clint went to the hotel. He learned that Dennis and Besford were now accompanied by a Carlos Samosa, Panamanian, from Veraguas. They were headed in that general direction. Santiago again. Clint was learning he could get as tired of driving as he did of buses.

Santiago, and they might have passed through. Wanda thought she saw Gordos's taxi at The Pyramid half an hour or so ago. The girl at the cash drawer at the restaurant in The Pyramid said they stopped for about ten minutes. One of them jumped on the bus for Panamá City that was just leaving. The other two, a dark man and a blond man, left with the taxi. She didn't see which way they went.

The Latino man was the one who caught the bus. He was carrying a suitcase and a maleta. She noted that, because people seldom used both. One or the other, usually only a maleta for the Panamanians. Clint decided that most probably meant Veraguas, but why did the Veragueno go toward Panamá City?

Only way to find out was to go to Veraguas. Clint had a decent meal at The Pyramid, spoke with several friends en route from David to Panamá City, then got in his car and headed for Veraguas. This kind of legwork (okay, bus and car-work) was what ninety percent of detective work amounted to. At least he was learning something this time. That wasn't always the case.

Clint parked at the little La Tipica Restaurant in Veraguas, got out of the car, stretched, swore, and went inside. There were only two patrons this time of the afternoon, so he was able to talk with the owner for a bit. He knew who Gordo was. He came there a lot, but he didn't know why, other than fares. The businessmen in Santiago would take a taxi instead of the bus. It wasn't that much and was faster and more pleasant. It was more status to arrive somewhere in a taxi.

Clint was *not* going to drive anymore, today! He asked about the best hotel in the moderate price range. He was told the owner, Samuel Amorosa, had three rooms that he rented right there. Air conditioning and cable TV, though the hot water was turned off, this time of the year. The water came from the tank at a reasonably comfortable temperature. Electricity for commercial was expensive.

Clint preferred a cool shower, so took the $21.00 room. It was surprisingly comfortable and was close to everything. There was a popular night club about two blocks away. Shopping was from there on into the centro.

Clint cleaned up, rested for an hour, then went to the bar. It seemed to be the most popular one in this part of Veraguas. Gordo and the two Canadians were sitting at the bar. The taxi was outside. There wasn't anything in it.

Confront them? Call in the police? Wait and watch?

He decided to wait and watch. He'd try to start a conversation. He took a stool next to Gordo, nodded to the three, then said, "I think I saw you in Almirante, at the dock near the water taxi, a few days ago. You were with a girl from Ireland?"

"Uh! Er, that is, we went to Bocas for a night," Besford answered. "We weren't much impressed. Shannon, the girl, stayed. We decided we'd see the rest of Panamá."

"Yeah. Bocas is the kind of place you either like or don't. It's a party town, what with the surfers and backpackers," Clint said. "I kind of like it for a few days at the time, then want to go elsewhere.

"You just left her out there? You weren't traveling together?"

"Oh, no! We met her in Changuinola. She said she came to Panamá via Sixola. That was her first stop. She was going to Bocas the next day, we were going to Bocas the next day, so we sort of went there together. She was a sort of strange one!" Dennis said. It sounded rehearsed to Clint. They'd made up a story to tell. They'd stick to it. Gordo even said she'd ridden in his taxi from Changuinola to David with them. She did seem a little strange. She promised to pay her part of the ride, then stuck it to the guys. They ended up paying for her.

"She was really a bitch on wheels!" Besford said, sourly. "She'd be your best friend, then stick you in the ass! She, uh, used us to find a place to stay and get meals cheap and all that, then takes off with some black rasta dude she met in that little bar by the bus station in Almirante!"

"Taxi? You say you drove a taxi from here to Changuinola? I'll bet that was some fare!" Clint said to Gordo.

"I, er, that is, took a couple of people in the development business there. Two hundred twenty dollars! I was going to ask two hundred, one of them said they would pay that, and not a penny more, so I acted like I might or I might not, then agreed. These people were coming here, anyway, and I didn't have a return fare, so I only charged them fifty. It was found money for me.

"As a driver, never tell anyone what you'll pay. Ask the cuenta, then bargain a bit for that kind of trip.

"I saw you drive in, so I know I'm not giving the stick to another taxi."

Clint laughed. He said he'd learned that bit a long time ago. He chatted with them a bit, then talked to a pretty girl who accompanied him back to his room. It was a great night!

In the morning, Clint went to the restaurant downtown near the bus terminal. It was the only place open at five thirty. He had hojaldres, bolitas, and coffee, and chatted with the woman running the place. There were only a few Indios there that early. She was suspicious of them. Clint said they were the only people he trusted, as a group. There were a few rotten apples, but that was true of any group of people. He managed to sound like he was just chatting, but she got the point. Clint didn't have patience with bigots.

He soon went to the table where four of the Indios were sitting, and said, "Coin dega! Tica Clint." (Good morning. I am Clint)

One of them grinned and said, in excellent English, "That is Ngobe. We speak a little different dialect here. Good morning. I am Solbiero, this is Tomas, this is Sandros, and this is Fredrico."

"I'm a detective," Clint said, knowing the best way to get along with anyone is to be up-front and yourself. "I'm interested in some people who came in yesterday. Gordo, the fat taxi driver, and two Canadians with him."

"Gordo is a shithead and a ladron," Sandros said, in not-as-good English. "If they came with him, they are not to be trusted."

"I figured as much. I just want to know what they're up to here. I think they killed a woman in Bocas.

"Do you know what may have been the reason Gordo went to Bocas with the woman?"

"The red-haired lady? She lived with him a week or so. They had some kind of plan about something. She is the dead woman?"

Clint nodded. "We'll speak Spanish, if any of you don't speak English. Do you know anything at all about her?"

"She met with a man in Santiago a lot and with Juan Ysalas, the lawyer. They had some kind of thing. The man from Santiago came twice to see her. The lawyer brought some legal papers," Sandros answered.

"She met with Aldo once. He went to the house while she was the only one there. He stayed an hour," Fredrico said. "We work in the finca that is all the way around the place he stays, if you wonder why we know so much about them."

They chatted awhile. Clint ordered a large plate of hojaldres and large coffees for everyone. They seemed good people, not unlike the Ngobe, but different, in some ways. They were intelligent, as most of the Indigenos were.

Clint had another few things to research when they left for work. He knew where Gordo's house was. He knew the finca all around grew crops and pastured cows in rotation of the fields. The four were the managers of the whole finca, which was something over 500 hectares in size. The barns and storage sheds were behind and to one side of Gordo's place.

Clint went back to the restaurant/inn where he was staying for a second light breakfast and to chat with the one couple who were staying in the rooms. They were from Germany. They came every year. They were partners in a small ranch they had financed with an Indio family. It was doing very well for the area. It paid for their yearly vacation and the Indio family were very well-off by local standards. It was so very seldom things worked out well for everyone in a deal, anymore. Very sad world we live in.

After the breakfast he asked Amoroso if he knew the lawyer, Ysalas.

He shrugged. "He's a lawyer. What can I say?"

"One of those?"

Samuel grinned. "They're all 'one of those.' It's what a lawyer is. I don't suppose he's worse than the rest, but he's not better, either. If his lips are moving, he's lying."

Clint found where his office was and strolled around town awhile. He dropped into the office about eleven, but the girl said he was working on a case where he must be in Panamá City for two more days.

He ran into Besford at the hardware store. He said "Hello." Besford was buying welding rod and plate steel. He said he had to make a security door or everything they had would end up disappearing a little at the time. Clint said that was a problem in any of the Latin American countries. The people didn't have much. They would take anything that wasn't welded down – even that, at times. Locks didn't mean much when the more practiced thieves were in the area, though he didn't think many of them were here. More in parts of Panamá City and Colon. Costa Rica was getting bad, but Panamá was very much safer, both from violence and theft.

Besford agreed that Costa Rica was impossible anymore. San Juan was now as bad as Limon always had been.

They parted. Clint grinned. So this one had spent some time in Costa Rica. Sergio could get any information they might have on him and his friend. Shannon was supposed to have come from Costa Rica, according to what had been said – but she did *not* come through Sixola. That probably meant Frontera. Sergio could check that. He probably already had. Clint called him to find they had all been reported about in Costa Rica. Dennis had been in some trouble when some thugs tried to rob him. He'd put two of them in the hospital with various broken bones. It had been determined that he was merely defending himself from robbery. He was released without charges.

Clint went to a little tienda on the corner of the road into the finca, where Gordo was staying. After about an hour and a half the taxi went by toward Veraguas. The three were together. Clint decided it might be a good time to snoop around. He had left the car at the inn and taken a taxi to the tienda. It was about a kilometer and a half to the house. Fifteen minutes. If he had half an hour he could be in and look around, then go to chat with his four friends of this morning if it looked like he may be found there.

The place was between just livable and semi-Okay. It wasn't clean. There was a lot of trash in the yard. Clint watched for a few minutes, then went to the door to knock and call out "Buenas!" No one answered.

He could see Fredrico and Sandros working on a fence on the far side of a shed. He managed not to be seen by them as he went to the side of the house and into a small attached bodega. There was a door from the bodega into the house that was left open (if you used a little device often seen on TV detective shows).

The inside was dark. There were heavy cloths and flattened cardboard cartons covering the windows. There was still enough light that he didn't need more than the light from his celular, now and then.

They had built a steel safe with three large padlocks holding the heavy lid down. It was tightly welded along all the seams. Clint estimated it would weigh about eighty pounds, empty, and it was more than he could do to lift one corner an inch off the floor. He didn't find anything else, except some letter from Ysalas and a lawyer in Panamá City.

He heard the taxi coming along the rough road and waited until it was parked in front to leave through the bodega, climb the fence onto the finca, and stroll over to the entrance road to call out to Sandros and Fredrico. He said he wanted to see the place, to see where Gordo lived in case he needed to come there. The taxi was parked out front, so he supposed that was the place.

Sandros winked at him. He had seen him. Fredrico said that was the place.

They chatted as the two went to the shed with their

tools. Solbiero and Tomas joined them with their own tools. They locked everything up and went out front where a rusty old GMC truck took them all back into Veraguas.

He was at least partly right in his assumptions. That there was something taken, probably cash and precious metal bars, from that little reef, Shannon was killed. The stuff was now in Veraguas, at Gordo's place.

Gordo, Besford, Dennis, and Ysalas were in on it. Minimum.

How did Shannon O'Brien fit? What was her connection?

To learn what was really going on, Clint would have to track things from her. She was, somehow, the key to the whole thing.

He stayed for the night, then headed back toward Santiago, thought a bit, and went on to David. He called Sergio and Judi to find anything they knew about O'Brien, then caught a plane to San Jose'. That was the only place he might find information about her. She had stayed there for two months, according to her passport.

The bar where the Canadien met them, The Red Lantern, had a few tourists and five or six locals. They weren't, any of them, the kind of people Clint would trust farther than he could throw the bar. It was seedy, but much of San Jose' is anymore. He had a $2.50 beer, which he sipped slowly. No one seemed interested in him – except when he paid for the beer. Two of them saw him change a twenty. He smirked to himself and said he was going to the hotel. Maybe he'd be back tomorrow, maybe he'd find a place more to his liking.

He went out and turned left, toward a darker street. He saw the two from the corner of his eye as he turned into the street. He stepped behind a large croton. The two came looking for him. He stepped out, acting like he'd stopped to piss. They converged on him from either side. One pulled out a long switchblade. He said, "Dinero, gringo!' The other said, in English, "You pay or die!"

He stepped to the side and grabbed the arm with the switchblade in the hand, twisted it behind him until he screamed, then chopped him in the neck. He dropped like a bag of wet sand. Clint turned toward the other, who was starting to run down the street. Clint was faster. He caught him and gut-punched him. He went to his knees, retching.

"An answer or two, ladron, or you die here!" he snapped. The hood gasped and sobbed.

"Who met with the Irish woman a week or so ago in that bar?"

The hood gasped and shook his head. Clint grabbed him by the hair, jerked his head back, and slapped him. Hard.

"I asked a question!"

"Two guys from Canada! Jimmy and Chuck! Surfers or something! They met right there. She said she saw one of them in Ontario at some place with someone, a godfather, and wanted to talk to them about a proposition!"

"Before they came?"

"Just Nikolo, the Russian mafia guy. She lived with him a month or so. He was pissed when she left. He said she was a thief. She took his papers or something. Maybe his passport. He was that pissed."

Clint let him go and walked off. That may be his connection. He had to find Nikolo.

He went to two other low-class places to find what he could about Nikolo. It seemed he stayed at a private home a short distance above town. Nobody went there. It was dangerous. Lots of people knew him, none claimed friendship.

Good enough! Clint went back to the hotel and sacked out.

In the morning, Clint had a decent breakfast, then headed out of town to the house described. He went to the gate and called out, getting an answer from a call box by the gate, but under a branch. He was asked what he wanted.

"I have to speak with Nikolo. I'm Clint Faraday, from Bocas, Panamá."

"What does Bocas have to do with me?"

"They got your stash and have it in another place. They killed the O'Brien woman."

There was a pause, then a large bullish man came from the house with a key to open the gate.

"Nikolo?" Clint asked.

"Huh-uh. He's in the house. You carrying?"

"No."

He nodded and led Clint into the house, where another man, not quite so large, greeted him. He told Viktor, the first, to bring coffee and whatever their guest desired.

"I've heard of you or you would not be in this house. Armokov? Panamá City?"

"Vasily? He's between an acquaintance and a friend. We had some dealings. We get along pretty well. I'm up-front and don't play those games. He liked that. He said he always knew exactly where I stand at all times."

"And you come here to announce that the fucking bitch is dead and my ... stash, you called it ... is gone. That's as up-front as it gets! I can see why Vasily respects you so!

"Talk about somebody who is *never* up-front with *anybody* and you've got that backstabbing bitch, dead to rights!

"Where is the property?"

"I'll tell you if it'll make things any easier or better in Panamá. We don't want anymore of this kind of thing screwing up the lives of innocent people. If only your bunch is involved and things will be handled outside of Panamá I'll tell you.

"What's it about? How much cash and how much other?"

"The cash isn't important. It was only included so that our people wouldn't have a lot of trouble moving the rest of it. It was something over two million. There are fifteen bars of platinum, fifteen of gold, and a lot of silver. There are about three and a half kilos of uncut emeralds and two kilos of best-grade diamonds."

Clint figured. "Two kilo bars?"

"Yes."

"Two to three hundred million."

"We don't sell that cheap. Five. The emeralds are historic artifacts or whatever they call them. The shipment was made to that figure."

"How will you handle it if I tell you where it is?"

"Will it stay there for a time?"

"I think definitely so. They don't want to dump any of it on the regular market while you're still watching so close. They'll spend some of the cash. Can you trace that?"

"Of cou... Okay. No. You're up-front with me, I am with you. We have no way to follow that cash. It wasn't enough to worry about. That was jst plain stupid! It won't happen again!

"You see, now I understand that it is something to

worry about – not for itself, but for where it can later lead you. I will not give you an answer you want to hear. I am not the only person involved – another stupidity!

"I will consult with my partners, such as they are, and try to convince them it would be better to bide our time than to rush into something that will only cause later grief. None of us are, as you gringos say, hurting for money."

"This is just a game? A diversion?"

He laughed. "More or less. I do it for reasons such a person as you would probably not understand."

"You have no friends. You are bored with life and try to find something to cause at least a temporary pause in that boredom."

"You are amazing! I fear you are also correct. Perhaps I can find that friend in you?

"You see, I know not another person I can trust without very serious reservations. I feel I can trust you."

"Unless I'm also playing a game?"

"No. You are not. That is a thing you would not have stated, were it so."

"You know something? I think we could be friends. Vasily is a lot like you. Is he a partner?"

"Not in this. He seeks adventure in various other places."

Clint nodded. "Well, I'll be in touch." He handed Nikolo a card with his e-mail and celular number. Nikolo wrote a number on a piece of paper and said it would reach him anytime. Don't allow anyone to know it.

Clint glanced at it and crumpled the paper. Nikolo raised an eyebrow. "It's memorized. If it's not around on a piece of paper, it won't go anywhere else." He told him the number.

"A good talent to have. I can do it, a little. Come by anytime, my friend. You will always be a welcome guest in my home.

"I have never before said that! To anyone!"

"Could I ask how O'Brien got the, er, information?"

"Another very stupid thing by me. She was a whore on the make. I brought her here. That is a diversion I can enjoy at which she was very expert. She found a paper that was in a book (he pointed to a large mahogany cabinet with hundreds of books) because my safe can be entered with little trouble by a person trained in such things. I read extensively in six languages. I didn't know anyone who ever came here would know Aramaic. She did, and was looking through a book while I was outside at the pool, apparently, and found the papers. There is no safe place to hide anything, I fear."

"They were maps?"

"And a list of the contents."

"*That* wasn't smart! I have to say it before you do."

"Partly true. They were not in the same book or books in the same language. The other set was in Canton Chinese. I doubt she found those because she read the language. Even I don't read it. She found the list in the Aramaic book. I think there was a reference of some kind about the location maps, so she searched and found it. I don't see when she had the time. It was in a different section of the case."

"She could eliminate Spanish, English, French, and Russian languages, German ... it didn't take long."

"How could she ... I see! It would be obvious that it would not be in any book anyone coming here might look at! It would occur to her that Aramaic wasn't a language anyone might understand here."

"The first thing a detective would think," Clint agreed.

"And a lesson to be learned. Where would you recommend?"

"Religious works. Nobody who comes here would waste their time looking through those!"

He laughed again. "I think I really do like you, Clint Faraday. It is refreshing beyond belief to find someone who isn't a phony-ass."

Clint laughed. He said he thought they really could be friends. He went back to the hotel and checked out, then headed for the airport.

Of course, he knew full-well that Nikolo was playing a game – but maybe they could still be friends. It had happened with several unexpected people, already. That was from being pragmatic about life. It's not like you want it to be, it's like it is.

Clint got off the plane in David and got his car, then drove to Dave's apartment to put things together without a lot of distraction. He knew there was a lot missing.

Where did the stuff come from? Laundering was out, for this. That bunch laundered money by the millions per day.

Was the other content stolen? From whom?

Clint thought a bit, then called Manolo, an undercover agent for Interpol and various other organizations. He would put out feelers to find if some bigshot drug lord or whatever was looking for something or someone. Stolen jewels and gold would very definitely be looked for by Interpol, if it was even partly legitimate. Nikolo said there was jewelry with historic importance, so that would definitely be investigated by Interpol.

He called Manny Mathews, who said he hadn't heard anything. He'd put out feelers.

Clint could make a short rundown of events:

Nikolo and partners got the stuff (?) and put it in safe boxes to hide under a small coral reef off of Dolfin Point to wait until they could safely dispose of it. He – and they, according to him – didn't need money. It was a lark to try to get some excitement into their dull lives. That, more than likely, meant it was taken from a big drug lord or someone in an illegitimate business of some type. Shannon O'Brien found the maps and descriptions when she shacked up with him for a week or so. O'Brien had run into two men she had met in Canada who were running with the scumbag crowd. She met them again in San Jose' among the scumbag crowd there, and made a deal where they would all end up with millions. She came to Panamá, where she found a shady all-around scumbag in Veraguas. She made a deal. She contacted Besford and Dennis and said to meet her in Changuinola. She took the taxi there. They rented a sports boat in Almirante, went to the place her maps showed, got the treasure – and something went wrong. He could figure she tried to put the screws to her partners. She had the reputation of using people and turning on them.

How did they manage to get that weight into the boat? Two boxes that would have weighed nearly three hundred pounds apiece, if he calculated right.

They were certainly big enough. They did take them onto the taxi in Almirante.

Okay. She picked the wrong place to try to put the screws to them. The problem was solved right there.

The problem with *her* was solved right there. There's still a huge problem. Nikolo and partners.

Clint could surmise that was what O'Brien had tried. "I get half and you three split the other half or I tell the Russian mafia who and where you are." Exit the lovely Shannon O'Brien, downstage left. Her continuing part was now written out of the play.

So. He could work with that, could probably prove it, definitely could prove it, with that steel lockbox in Gordo's house. That would tell Nikolo who and where. It could get too damned hairy with that bunch. He wished he could trust Nikolo enough to make a deal with him to keep it out of Panamá, but knew the deal would be they would keep it out of Panamá only so long as it didn't inconvenience them. Nikolo had hinted that he would go along, but that his partners may not. That was why the wait, now.

Clint sighed. There wasn't much he could do until he

had a call from Nikolo. He headed for Bocas.

"Nothing much is happening here," Sergio said, when Clint went to the police station to report what he'd found. "It seems everything was from somewhere else.

"Should I have an arrest warrant waiting when you're ready to present the case? I can keep it quiet, I suppose."

"You can if you can be certain Nikolo or they can't know anything about it."

"I'll see. Maybe yes, maybe no."

They chatted awhile, then Clint went home. Judi was just coming into town. She saw him. She waved and said she would be home about five thirty. He saluted and went on in to check his e-mail, then cooked a good meal of corvina with hush-puppies and mustard greens.

He cleaned off his deck and lazed around for a little while until Judi came to say she was really getting a workout with the various committees she was on. She liked that. It kept her busy. She didn't have any other gossip. It was sort of dead in Bocas except for the surfers and party crowd.

They went to the Rip Tide for a meal and to talk with the regulars and a few tourists, then Clint went home to sack out. Tomorrow would be busy – or not.

In the morning he had his hojaldres and coffee on the deck, then puttered around his boat. He got in the water with scuba gear and cleaned the hull, then the engine, then the interior. It was spotless when he was through at three twenty. His phone buzzed. He noted the number on the ID, so answered. Manny said there wasn't a hint of anything as big as this, so it wasn't connected with any mob, anywhere – unless Nikolo's bunch brought their own mob into it. No one was looking for them for anything beyond the ordinary.

Manolo called to say there wasn't anything nearly like what Clint described Interpol was interested in. There was a slight hint that someone on some island had lost something big, but there wasn't anything much known about it. It wasn't in Panamá or the waters nearby, so far as he could tell. It was some private agents who had asked that he keep a lookout for lost emeralds. They didn't really believe that Panamá was involved, but were covering all the bases.

Judi came over to say that there was some big dignitary coming in tonight or tomorrow on his private plane. Sergio was pissed, because he was supposed to protect such people. This was one he didn't want any dealings with in any way. He thought the fact he had more money than god would let him buy his way out of anything.

"One of those gringo developers who leave it up to everyone else to live down to what they are?"

"No, not a gringo. I think he's a sheik or prince or something. He owns a whole country or whatever in the Mediterranean."

"Why the hell would he come here?"

"You got *me*! There's nothing anyone like that could want here!"

Clint shook his head. Too many like that came to Bocas. It almost never bode good for the gringos. Maybe this one was an Arab or something where the gringos wouldn't be in the same stereotype. He could hope.

Manolo said an island? One not near Panamá? I wonder!

The private jet was just able to land on the runway in Bocas Town. The pilot and co-pilot and two men in expensive suits got off. The one, somewhat fat and definitely Arabic, seemed to expect everyone to bow to him or something. Clint managed to be walking toward the gate when they reached it. The bigshit's companion said, "Stand back!"

"Fuck you," Clint returned, pleasantly. "Who you may be somewhere else doesn't mean pigshit here."

"You don't know with whom you trifle!" he spat.

"Neither do you, apparently. Difference is, I don't give a flying shit. Don't give me another order or I'll dump your ass right here!"

He didn't know what to say. "If you were in another place you would be down on your knees pleading for your life now!"

"We ain't in another place. You'll follow our rules here and maybe we'll follow your rules there. All you cruds are here is another bunch of obnoxious egocentric arrogant tourists who were raised in a barn and bleat like farm animals."

The bigshot was pretending to be amused. "I think I like your courage. If you ever are in need of a very well-paying job in another place, call on me. Yusef will give you my number. I am Ali el Mika'h Mikim."

Clint stepped back and waved him through the gate, but made the others wait there until he went through, which amused Mikim even more.

Mikim and Yusef went toward a waiting car. Clint recognized the Japanese thug, Itumi, as the waiting passenger in the car. He got out and bowed slightly to

Mikim, who said something that made him laugh. He looked over to Clint and smirked. Clint could figure what that was about. He'd be ready for them.

It also tied another few things together. He thought about it. He wondered again about some things.

He called Nikolo and asked if he knew Mikim was in Bocas.

There was a long pause. "You amaze me. How did you find out about King Ali the Less Than Magnificent so quickly?"

"Easy. He has four men here looking for the stuff. He just flew in on that jet and pulled the visiting royalty act. Two and two is still somewhere in the neighborhood of four.

"Does this mean what I think it means?"

"That the bitch knew who we meant? Probably. She read Aramaic, which should have warned me. She was always double-dealing everyone. He probably came there to collect his, as you call it, stuff, in a deal with her.

"Clint, it is only a very small part of what he has stolen from his people. You can't know the depth of horror of living in constant fear such a person visits upon his so-called subjects. Now I must wonder if she told him about me."

"I really do doubt that," Clint mused. "She would be the type to hold that power over him to guarantee her own safety. She could say he would learn that after she had her cut and was gone.

"You know something? I think I know why she's dead!"

"Yes. She tried to hold King Ali over her partners' heads. She was stupid enough to let them know she was playing that side of the street, too. They would know she hadn't told about them. That meant they could get away with the whole thing by getting rid of her. All they would need was a day or two to disappear. He wouldn't have any way to find them without her."

"So they played her game on her. I think she let something slip to Gordo. Now he's made a deal or two on the side. Lovely bunch!"

"I can't be flippant about this, quite yet. He has enough money to buy almost anything."

"He just thinks he does."

"Yes. There is not enough money ever printed to buy you. For this fact alone you have my deepest respect. I will ask that you, under no circumstances, tell him about me."

"And vice versa. I'll see what I can do. I think he's already ordered that I be killed or seriously injured or something. I refused to step aside to let him through the airport gate and called him an obnoxious pig, or something such. He acted amused and offered me a job if I ever needed one – but his eyes weren't in the least amused. He wanted to have a way to reach me."

"Be most careful, my friend. Do not underestimate him, as he will undoubtably do about you."

"I'll certainly remember that!"

They chatted a minute more, then Clint headed for his house. The car that Itumi was using was sitting in front of the gate. That was unexpected. Clint thought they'd wait until he was alone after dark or something. He strolled unconcernedly to his gate and looked into the car. They had Judi.

"So? What's the deal to be, pukeface?" he asked. "Holding Judi is about as stupid as I thought you were from the first."

"I want to know a few things about a woman named

Shannon Elizabeth O'Brien," Mikim said, from the back seat. "Miss Lum will not be harmed in any way should you wisely choose to cooperate."

Judi grinned. "Isn't it exciting? I get kidnapped again! I'm going to have to start charging you piecemeal if this doesn't stop. It could get boring."

"Well, I suppose they have to try *something*," Clint replied. "If they'd checked around they could see how far this will get them.

"Oh! Did Marko return my call? I've been so busy I forgot to turn the phone on."

"Marko? No." She looked at him quizzically. "Why would he call? Some DEAL I'm not in?"

"Oh, he's living not too far from Ali Baba, here. I think he'll be amused by the abject stupidity of messing with his friends."

"Who is this Marko?" Mikim demanded. "Itumi said you were friends with such a person, and that might cause serious problems for us."

"Marko Bocinni? He's a friend from the states," Judi said. "He's living in the Mediterranean on an island somewhere ... Oh! You're from that part of the world, right?"

The three chattered at each other in Aramaic – or something. Yusef trying to explain something to Mikim, who was trying to get some answers from Itumi, who was arguing with Yusef. It was almost comical.

"Oh, well. Come on in, Judi. I've got some lobster chowder in the 'fridge. We can throw a green salad together. I'd invite the rest of you, but you aren't the kind of people who would ever be welcomed into my home."

Judi grinned and opened the door. She got out, and said, "Thank you for your hospitality. I hope I can return it in kind some day – if I ever decide to frequent the gutter."

Mikim looked like he could bite through a steel bar. Yusef didn't know what to do. Itumi threw his arms up and said something. The driver started the car and drove off. Judi and Clint had a giggling fit. They went inside and had lobster chowder and a lettuce, pineapple, and pear salad.

It was still not quite coming together. Clint had a large collection of facts that seemed to follow a pattern and timeline, but something critical was missing. It didn't seem logical Nikolo and company would choose this kind of situation to pull this kind of deal on. There had to be more. A lot more. There must be something in the stuff in Gordo's house that would cause Mikim problems serious enough that he was here in person. He wasn't the type to handle anything himself. He would hire anything he wanted less serious. His attitude was, like Sergio suggested, that he could buy his way into or out of anything. He'd already had a shock or two about how far that would go with some of the people here!

Clint looked over to see Dave and Ben on Judi's deck with her. He waved and they waved back. Dave held up a plant with a flower that, as much as Clint could see from the distance, was a dark violet color, rather unusual in orchids. Dave pointed to Clint's left. He had one blooming right there on his deck. It had opened just this morning, apparently. He waved and got out his camera for a picture. It was different.

He then went into town to talk with Sergio. King, as Nikolo had labeled him, Ali the Less Than Magnificent and friends were staying at the Tropical Suites, where they were making pains in the asses of themselves. True to form. Only Itumi seemed embarrassed by them. Yusef didn't seem to be able to understand that he couldn't give orders to people here.

Clint went on the half block to the police station and saw Doc, the ME for the island, was in Sergio's office. It was a bit tense. Clint asked why.

"There was a knife fight or something such out near the bombas at Saigon, past your place. Two men are dead. No one can tell why they would be involved in anything like that. They're very peaceful people. Pacho Roberto and Orlando Smith."

"They're friends!" Clint exclaimed. "They're never violent in any way. They get drunk and fight each other, but that's just for fun. The macho thing."

"Exactly," Doc said. "I knew them both, well. We had a beer or two together, sometimes. The Indigenos are *not* violent. They would *not* be involved in any knife fights."

"What's the ... how do you figure?" Clint asked.

"That sheik or king or prince or whatever was out there earlier," Sergio answered, sourly. "His buddy, the Yusef character, got into a shoving match with several of the Indios, Pacho and Lando among them. The witnesses say it was because they wouldn't get out of the way where king shithead wanted to go."

"Check on the others involved in the shoving!" Clint cried.

"They weren't that local. They were from Solarte, so they weren't around last night or this morning," Sergio said. "We can't find any way to prove anything! I want those people out of here!"

"I think you have evidence enough to put the bunch of them in a cell for awhile – while you get them deported as undesirables," Clint suggested. Doc agreed, wholeheartedly.

"I'd better take an army with me," Sergio said. "It could turn into a little war."

"Their choice!" Doc snarled. "Do they have diplomatic immunity? He *is* a king."

Sergio checked the passport records. He noted the

visas. "No. No immunity. They came here on business visas."

"Stupid!" Clint said. Doc high-fived him.

"Want to come along?" Sergio asked.

"Wouldn't miss it!" Clint returned.

There were four officers in the station. Sergio called for six more to come in, armed them all with automatic weapons, then they walked over to the Tropical Suites. Mikim and company were not there at the moment. The employees of the hotel said they would assist the police in any way to get rid of those slimeball bastard hijos de putas.

They checked around to find the bunch were at the airport. The police squad got in the truck and headed for there. They arrived just as the jet was taxiing down the runway for takeoff. Sergio had the flight control officer demand they return to the terminal. They took off hurriedly – except Itumi and three others, who were trying to be inconspicuous. Clint pointed them out. Sergio had them arrested on the spot and taken to the station. They were thinking of resisting, but that would have been suicide. They very damned well knew it.

They were being taken to cells when Itumi demanded to know what charges they were being held on.

"Suspicion," Sergio said.

"Of what?" he demanded.

"Being low-life trash. I don't need anything more than the fact that every damned one of you were carrying unpermitted weapons. If any of those knives have a sign of blood from Orlando or Pacho, you will be charged with murder as a group, and will spend twenty years in carcel. I hope to have that evidence before King Fuckhead manages to leave. He and the pleasant and accommodating Yusef can join you."

"He's a king! You can't put him in any jail! We know that much!" one of the hoods cried.

"He's here on business visa. We can and will put his obnoxious ass in a cell!" Clint said. "Let's see him try to order that bunch at the prison in Panamá City around. That should be a real hoot."

"He'll soon buy his way around them," Itumi said, confidently.

"The wardens? Probably. The other inmates? With his attitude? Gimme a break! He won't live a day!" Clint replied. "I don't think any of you will last very long. Don't start any long novels."

They were led out and to cells. Doc came rushing in. Sergio handed him the knives and guns in their plastic sealed containers.

"One drop of blood, O-positive!" Sergio said.

"One ADN chain," Doc replied, and rushed out. That he came for the evidence, personally, said a hell of a lot about how he felt about this bunch.

Clint talked a bit. He went home as soon as they received word that the jet was in Panamá City, where he was being held. Mikim was making all sorts of demands and giving everyone around him orders. They had to have four large officers carry him, bodily, to a cell, where he was screaming like a spoiled four-year-old.

Clint shook his head and grinned. Mikim was about to learn exactly how far his royalty went in Panamá.

Clint thought about this all the way to his place. Something was a long way out of kilter with the whole thing. It was an almost logical progression, but there was a stgrong feeling that something much more sinister was behind it. There was something in that stuff that would cause ... what? What was Mikim so scared of?

Clint didn't want to have an armed squad go into

Gordo's house just yet, but he didn't see any other way to handle it. He called Manny and asked if there was someone he could use here to get that safe box.

"Don't go off half-cocked!" Manny said. "What are you looking for?"

"I don't know. There has to be something there that King Fartface doesn't dare let get out!"

"That you wouldn't recognize if it was on the table right in front of you now?"

"I don't know what to do, Manny!"

"Maybe you should study about the history of Mikim and Nikolo? Find out where their paths crossed? Find the real story behind this crap act they're pulling?

"I've had some checks made on Mikim. He's got a little sheikdom on a Mediterranean island and has declared himself king through right of progression. His father and grandfather were sheiks who owned the island. It's six miles by eight. There's an oil transfer on one end. It's deep enough that the big tankers can go in close. That's what gave him the idea. His father and uncles built the transfer. It's making about two million a day for him. I can send you the whole thing. It's a lot of boring reading."

They agreed to that. Maybe Clint could find a reason for what was happening now in the past. He left the computer on the scrambled receive program with Manny and went calling on the families of Pacho and Orlando. He promised them he would see the ones behind the murders caught and prosecuted. He had one idea about that, now. It was based on the fact Mikim thought he could buy his way out of anything.

He would wait a few more days. That would soften Mikim up about right. Clint didn't doubt Doc would find some blood on one of those knives. It was as much as impossible to get all of it out of an iron-based metal. All they needed was one DNA chain to make it a solid conviction. Seeing it was done under orders by paid assassins, they were all equally guilty here, in one section of the law.

He got home to find 123MB of information waiting for him. He groaned and brought up the file. It wasn't as bad as he'd thought. There were a lot of pictures, which increased the MBs tremendously. One high-resolution picture was as much as a hundred pages of print.

Pictures? Maybe a picture of something in that safe box?

He brought them up. There were pictures of all the royal jewels, with numbers. He decided to read as much as he could about the history, then would go to the pictures when he knew what – if anything – they meant.

The only connection he could find was that the jewels were the basis of the progression of the sheik or king. The one possessing the jewels passed them on to the next ruler when he died. It wasn't necessary that the one getting the rule was the eldest son, as in most cases of that kind of progression in that area. Clint had read about the progression, but hadn't noted much about it at the time. He went back and checked. Mikim's father was the second son of the former sheik, not the first. Mikim's uncle had died only weeks after the progression, having been in rather poor health at the time of the progression – which was two months after the old sheik died. The old sheik died of some kind of suspicious wasting. Many believed he was poisoned. The eldest son died in like circumstances. Mikim's father had the jewels because, according to him, his father knew his brother would be unable to rule. The sheikdom was in trouble, financially, but Mikim's father had a lot of personal money he invested in building the port facility. He saved the whole mess.

Mikim was always pampered and trained for rule. He was a despot the people despised, but couldn't do anything about. All three of his wives had escaped to England and Australia to get away from him with their children. He had a son and daughter by one and a daughter by another. The third didn't have any surviving children. She had a daughter, who died at birth.

Where did Mikim's father get enough money to bail the country out? It wasn't really that much by today's standards, but a couple of million dollars was a lot of money eighty years ago. What did that have to do with it?

The history seemed to hint that Mikim's father had killed his own father and brother to get the sheikdom. He already had plans to build that port. The oil companies would finance the port, no doubt. The family was as much as destitute – yet Mikim's father had enough to bail out the country? He had the money when he took over?

This didn't, as the old TV show kept saying, compute. Clint felt he knew why those jewels were so important. He called Manny and said he had enough to go on, now. He wanted that chest. He would also want an expert on identifying old jewelry. They had the papers, pictures, and identification specs on them.

"Okay. I read some of that stuff. I know how important that jewelry is. You think it will get Mikim out of the picture there, don't you?"

"I sincerely and deeply hope so."

"I'll arrange something."

Clint grinned to himself, then called Manny back to say to wait two days, then go for it.

Clint walked into the small dank interrogation cell in Panamá City to find Mikim sitting there, a bit thinner in just a few days, and declared, "You look like hell warmed over. They don't bow to you here, huh?"

"This is intolerable! I will bring an international incident against you! I *will not* live like this another day! I am royalty! I have immunity!"

"Then you should make arrangements for you to die today. You aren't going anywhere, probably for the next twenty years," Clint replied. "You don't seem to get it through your head that your money and position don't mean shit here. Your visa has to be diplomatic for that crap. Yours isn't. You can't get out of it, but you might be able to make it easier. All you have to do is have the families of the men you ordered killed not demand full prosecution."

He got a cunning look on his face. "Yusef told you I can buy my way out of this!"

"Not out, but not in so deep. Stay in the position you're in now, you go to the worst facility. Get a little pressure off the court, maybe you can make it one of the better places. It's the only concession they'll even consider. If you'd come here with a little respect for others you wouldn't be in the position you're in now. It's your own doing, so stop whining like a three year old spoiled brat before it's too late. Once the court declares conviction, you're gone. There won't be another chance."

"So! Why would you do anything to help me?"

"I wouldn't. I'm trying to help the families of two innocent and very good people that you had killed because you think you're more than the fatuous pig you are. They have a hard enough time just surviving without your type killing off their means of support."

He thought a moment. "I can make them drop the charges?"

"No. The charges are by the nation. You can maybe lessen the charges a small bit."

"And all I have to do is pay off the families and admit everything in court? Fuck off!"

"You don't have to admit anything. They've got you. When your hired assassin's knives had the blood of both victims on them you were as good as convicted. We don't care if you admit anything or not. It wouldn't make an iota's difference."

"You can't intimidate me!" he yelled. "Warden! Come here! This man threatened me!"

"Oh, drop the shit! There's a recorder sitting right there that says different. I take it you don't want to ameliorate your charges. Your choice. Have a nice day!"

He stood and started toward the door. Mikim said, "How much? Five million apiece? That should be enough for these kinds of animals."

"One million for both families – and the only animal here is you. Take it or leave it."

"I forgot how cheaply they can be bought. It comes from having too much. I can have my lawyer, such as he is, make a draw on my account for that small change."

Clint nodded. Mikim used his celular to call a lawyer, who would come with a withdrawal slip for Global Bank, if he wanted to use that account. He shrugged. The lawyer would be there in minutes. They waited.

The lawyer came in, presented the slip, had it witnessed by the two guards, and went with Clint to the bank to have the funds transferred to Clint's account in Banco Nacional de Panamá. Then Clint went home and called

Manny to say he could grab the safe box anytime. Manny said it would arrive by special carrier sometime before dawn in the morning. Dave's apartment in David.

Clint said that suited him. He called Dave, who was planning on going to David on the seven o'clock bus.

"We'll take my car. I'll probably be needing it in David," Clint suggested. Dave had no problem with that! They could leave earlier. Dave could stop in one place in La Fortuna where an orchid he thought might be a new species would be in bloom.

Clint grinned. He said that would be fine. They'd take his boat to Almirante. Half an hour.

"The chest wasn't there. It had been moved earlier, yesterday," Manny reported at five ten the following morning "I don't know how you'll find it, but I can see it doesn't go far from there. Gordo and the two Canadians are still there.

Clint thought a minute, then said he'd go on to Veraguas. He was on the way, anyhow. He told Dave and got in his car. He would be in Veraguas before noon. He had an idea about that box.

"Hi! I'm back!" Clint greeted Sandros and Fredrico. "Did you see when Gordo took the box out?"

"Hi, Clint! Yes, we helped them put it on the truck. It took all five of us. What's in it? Gold?" Sandros asked.

"Gold and jewels and silver and that kind of obvious thing," Clint answered.

"For truth?"

"Partly."

"So you want to know where they took it?" Fredrico asked, a small grin on his face.

"You didn't go with them to unload it?!"

"No, but I saw a map with a house marked."

"Ah! They didn't figure you'd have the intelligence to know what it was. They make too many wrong assumptions."

"It seems to have become a habit. The house is near Pocri. I don't know where, but very close."

"I never heard of Pocri. Where is it?"

"Inland from Las Tablas. On the other road."

"Going toward the Pacific," Clint mused. "They plan to get it out of Panamá. Thanks, guys. I'll probably be back before too long."

He got his car and took out his laptop to look up a map. Pocri was on a road to Las Tablas and to the main CPA (Pan American Highway). He could get there in about three hours.

Nothing else to do!

The drive wasn't so bad. It was an area Clint had never seen before, so he went slowly enough that he could look the area over. He figured Dave would want to go there. It was different enough that there would be a lot of plant life of the type he was researching.

Pocri is a typical small town. People are friendly and helpful. Clint soon found he was going to have to drive around the surrounding roads to find the house he wanted. Gordo hadn't come into town that they knew of.

Clint liked driving in new areas. He went along all the side roads toward the CPA. He found information in the small tiendas along the way. Four and a half hours later he found a woman running a little refrescos stand who said they stopped for sodas and galetas, then went down the rough road nearby. He had a Coke and cookies, chatted for a few minutes with the woman about David, then went carefully along the road, which was mostly a rocky cowpath. The house was half a kilometer in. No one was around. It looked abandoned, though it did have some very secure locks and the windows and doors had steel bar grates across them. Clint wouldn't be able to get in easily.

He thought for a few minutes, then called Manny to tell how to get to the place. Manny said there would be a man there within the hour who could get past any lock, anywhere.

Clint waited for an hour and a quarter, until a rickety old truck came up. Clint told the man driving he was waiting for a friend who said he had rented the place, but he didn't think he was going to show.

"Faraday? Marko B said you had to get inside a place that was pretty securely locked?

"I'm called Picks."

"That's it," Clint said, pointing toward the house. "I could use bolt cutters, but I'd rather get in and get what I want and get out again without anyone knowing how I got the stuff without doing anything like that."

He laughed and took a strange tool from the glove case and went to the front door steel grate. The lock was open in ten seconds, then he opened the lock in the inner steel door. They went in to find the safe box in the kitchen. Clint said the trouble was going to be moving the thing. It was heavy.

Picks used his celular and said, "Ten minute," to Clint.

Ten minutes later a car came in with four big men. They hoisted the box onto the truck, Clint made sure the locks were all back in place and that they hadn't left any signs they were there. They drove out through a little path/road to one side. They went through a field and onto the better road around a bend, where the woman in the tienda wouldn't know they'd been there. They stopped at a little restaurant, where Clint gave the four men in the car fifty dollars apiece. He said they'd never been within ten kilometers of that house they didn't know existed. They grinned and said they weren't in the habit of running their mouths. That was bad for business.

"I took a few seconds to look over the area, then got the Mapquest view enlarged until I could see that road where no one would see us coming or going. If the woman in the tienda saw you go in she'll wonder why you never came back out."

Clint nodded and told Picks where the box was to be delivered, if he knew a carrier they could trust.

"I'm to take it to David myself. Marko arranged everything."

Clint nodded. He said he'd try to be back to David before Picks, probably. He was going to go back and out the way he went in. He'd stop at the tienda to tell the woman he got stuck in a ditch and just got out. He never found anything before he came back.

He did that, then headed to David.

They unloaded the box and put it in the little Bodega at Dave's apartment. Picks opened all the locks on the box and said he wasn't interested in what was inside. Marko made that plain. Clint agreed and asked what he owed.

"You owe Marko, but he said he owes you more than he has. I wish I had a friend like that! He's living in Southern Spain, but let's it out that he's on an island in the Mediterranean. You know about that, so I'm not giving anything away. He said you're the safest person in the world to know that. You even know the house he's in, there."

"He's there part time and part time on the island. He has to make an appearance on the island every once in awhile so certain people won't be looking all over Spain and Portugal for him," Clint said. "I don't mind telling you what's in the box. It's money and gold and jewels."

"As heavy as it is, I guess that's true. Not any of my business."

Clint wished him well and went into the bodega to see what he could find. He was damned sure there was something in that chest that was important enough that some little tin king came in person to get it.

He carefully checked the items. There was, as Mikim said, almost two million in cash. Dollars. Apparently, Gordo, Besford, and Dennis had taken about ten thousand apiece. It was short of two million by thirty one thousand. The gold was there, as was the silver and platinum. There was a list that checked exactly to the items.

Clint studied the emeralds and diamonds. They seemed alright to him. He held the jewels that were the token of the ruler's progression. They looked exactly like the pictures he had from the net, and so forth. They were set in gold. It was heavy.

Clint didn't know enough. Manny would send an expert to check them over. There were marks that an expert could find that anyone else may miss. Not much else to do, so he locked up the bodega and went to a delicious dinner at Las Brasas. Manny's expert would be there at eight in the morning.

"Mr. Clinton Faraday? I'm Michael Foster. Mr. Bocinni has hired me to investigate some jewelry that is in your possession. I understand that this is to be kept very quiet, as it may have international repercussions should it be known the merchandise is in the hands of the government. You may place trust in me completely, as Mr. Bocinni will attest. You are to call him while I am here to confirm."

Clint invited him in, gave him a cup of coffee, and called Manny, who said Foster was as good an expert as there was and that he knew how delicate negotiations between governments could be. That was to let Clint know what to tell him and what not to tell him.

"If this is all authentic we can trust them. If not, we know what's behind it and can put a stop to a dangerous situation, Mr. Bocinni. All Panamá appreciates and respects your aid in this matter."

That done, Clint took Foster to the bodega, where he handed him the emeralds. Foster got a glance into the box and looked like his eyes would pop out of his head. He took the emeralds and frowned. "I can see why the suspicion! This is paste!"

That was a shock! Clint expected some kind of skulduggery, but not anything like this!

"You're positive?" he asked. "We couldn't tell, but you knew without making any tests?"

"I made a test when I picked them up. See?" He showed Clint a very small scratch on a facet of the largest emerald. "I do this to impress the impressible. This ring has a very sharp piece of corundum on the point here (a tiny needle-like projection) that will not affect true emeralds or diamonds, but will scratch glass and less hard things. It saves making delicate tests that are mostly for show. This is as good a copy as I've seen, so I can probably guess these were made between seventy and eighty eight years ago. In Egypt. One man was this good. This is the third piece of his work I've seen. The other two were items of importance to royalty in Europe. They had the copies made to be placed on public display while the genuine articles were placed in safer surroundings. They were legitimate. I can guess these are items some government wants to dispose of to raise money. They put them among these authentic items, such as the gold and platinum, to make it seem all was genuine.

"I like to imagine scenarios for these things. I won't tell anyone else anything at all, even that I was here in Panamá.

"Look at them through these." He handed Clint his glasses. Clint put them on and looked at the emeralds through them. There was almost no fire.

"Polarized. Paste doesn't reflect in the even forms that true jewels do. The absorption lines in these glasses are at different angles than regular polarized lenses, so catch the imperfections in jewelry as well as detecting artificial ones."

Clint thanked him and said he was to be careful to not let anyone know about this. It could cause such serious consequences to certain people that it could hardly be estimated.

He called Manny as soon as Foster was gone to tell him.

"So. His father sold the real jewels to get money to build that port, among other things. I still can't see what makes Mikim so afraid."

"I can," Clint replied. "It's in that history you sent me. It's in the wording."

"Gonna make me try to figure it for myself?"

"Oh, look at where the original progression was set. That constitution kind of thing that was guaranteed to hold forever. The part that says, 'So long as...'"

"I'll have to put this stuff somewhere. I'll be back home as soon as I can."

"I've put a search for that phrase. Here it ... 'So long as the original and authentic articles ...' Great exploding galaxies! He isn't the king if the original and authentic articles aren't in his possession! His father unintentionally sold the title with the emeralds!"

"Uh-huh. Now we have to see who does own all that stuff."

"I sincerely hope it'll revert to the people. There are about six thousand citizens, five thousand nine hundred living in poverty. Two million a day divided among them equally will make them all millionaires in a few months."

"Sounds good to me! Now I have to get this off of Panamá's back."

"Well, Judi, it looks like our recent guests will end up in the pen here for the next twenty. I'd like to get them out of this country, but it ain't a-gonner ever happen, I'm afraid. I want to try to get King Fartblossom home, if no one else. I think the stink we'll raise'll make them want to prosecute him – according to their own rules. Manny's having the laws there checked to see if we can manage to have the people own the country on a collective basis. Of course, it'll take about ten minutes for some crooked corrupt politicians to take it all back, I suppose.

"I want to know what to do with all that stuff in the chest."

"Ask Nikolo. Maybe you can find what's behind his end of it."

"I want to go see him. I think he wanted to get his hands on those emeralds. I want to see his face when I tell him they're paste copies of the real thing."

"That should be a classic!"

"I'm going to his place this afternoon. Maybe I can catch his expression on my camera phone."

They chatted a bit more, then Clint hung up and threw a few things in a bag for in case he had to stay away for more than the day. He locked the bodega after putting all the padlocks back on – except they were his padlocks, not the ones they took off.

He got in his car to head for the airport. He would be in Costa Rica until tomorrow, at least. His car could stay on the lot there.

The flight was a little rough, but not too bad. Clint checked into a hotel and took a taxi to Nikolo's house to announce himself at the gate. Viktor came to let him in. He'd called when he reached the airport. He wanted to see Nikolo before he had the chance to learn much about what had happened so far. He hoped to be able to arrange the handling of Gordo and the two Canadians without involving the Panamanian police. He wouldn't go so far as to allow them to be hit. He didn't think Nikolo would be that interested in them.

He was greeted warmly. Nikolo was out by his pool, enjoying a tall vodka collins, which he offered to Clint. Clint took one. It was real vodka, made from potatoes, not grain.

"So? What have we found so far?" Nikolo asked.

"Other than that the emeralds are paste copies and

Mikim and his goons are going to spend a few years in the lockup, not much. The fact the jewels are fakes means that Mikim and his father weren't kings or whatever."

Nikolo turned over his drink, then grinned. He said, "You enjoyed that, didn't you?"

"To be honest ... yes! I wish I had a picture of your expression!"

He got the finger. "That was much more than I had hoped. I wanted to be able to be rid of him, but I was planning to sell most of the stuff to finance a little private revolution when we had the organization set up properly.

"I can tell you about some of my partners, if what you say is true – and I would not doubt your word for one pico-second!

"You see, this was to be an overthrow of that one we call the Monster of the Med. It was arranged by two families who were once owners of much land in the place there is now a port. A port that makes two million dollars on an average day. It is not so much that they want the land back. They want that family brought down from the rule and dragged through the streets in disgrace. They would not object too greatly if the land were to be returned, but that is truly a secondary con-sideration."

"I want to arrange for the people to collectively own the whole island," Clint replied. "They'd be included in that if they're citizens. It would make a few thousand people living in abject poverty into millionaires in a few days, if the treasury is as bloated as I've heard. Billions in what amounts to stolen funds. I'd really like to see some way those people can select their own government, but realize things aren't done that way in that area.”

“Because a thing hasn’t been done does not mean it can’t be done. The ideas of democracies is gaining popularity. What we have to do is offer education to the people. It has been denied for some decades. They need a medical facility.

“We aren’t so bad as our reputation, in many things. We are worse in others. That I do not doubt. Perhaps we can arrange for our ex-king to be returned for the entertainment and pleasure of some few thousand people he has held in thrall and in poverty for his entire life?”

“That would be something I’d like to see, but no. They have to wait twenty years. He won’t survive twenty weeks in jail in Panamá. His attitude and tendency to give orders won’t bide well for his health and physical welfare.

“What do we do with all that crap in the chest?”

“I’d say to keep it as your fee, but also feel that’s not in my province to say.”

“How about sending it to the social reform party, which some of your betterminded partners just formed? It will be guaranteed that the proceeds are used to build schools and a medical center?”

He laughed. “I generally hate reformers. I don’t think I hate you. I rather like you. I do greatly respect you.”

“Can you set that up?”

“I will make honest effort. I will contact you when I have something to offer. That, or a counter-offer. I think, when I explain that it’s that or you keep the contents and use the funds in that manner here, there will be a concerted ‘Bravo!’ tendered to you.”

“If they’re sincere about that they won’t need that suggestion. It’ll tell you a lot about them and their motives as individuals.”

"I cannot and would not argue that."

"What can we do about the three who got me into this by killing O'Brien?"

"It was her. They were being used and turned on her the same way she turned on others. I couldn't care less about them. You arrange something. She received exactly what she'd earned and deserved."

Clint thought about it. He nodded, grinned, and changed the subject to the way Panamá was handling their soccer program. It seemed to be very effective!

Clint went back to the airport to learn he couldn't get a flight until tomorrow at eleven. He checked into a hotel and had a very good night in the restaurant/bar there.

"Sergio, remember how we handled that bunch with the land-theft scheme?"

"Which one? You had several of those."

"They started killing each other off. They were deported so that Panamá wouldn't be saddled with keeping them locked up for up to twenty years. We can do that with Besford and Dennis, can't we?"

He looked thoughtful. He, like Clint, didn't want Panamá to have to house and feed the type. He said he'd try to work it out. That would leave Gordo. He'd be convicted of complicity and would serve a couple of years.

Nikolo called to say Clint's suggestions about the reform were acceptable to all but one of them. That one would be removed from the group, as he had shown he was more interested in money and power, not in helping his own people. The people would learn, through a careless loss of a document, that he was exactly what he was. When they held elections, if that could actually be arranged, he need not apply for nomination as a candidate for anything.

"We do sound obsequious, don't we?" Nikolo finished.

"It's a good kind of obsequiety. I can live with that."

"We have the problem of delivery of the stuff without government knowledge nor intervention. There are many who are corrupt here, too."

"Easier to move it ... I'll make a few calls and call you back."

"That will be well, my friend. I will await your word."

Clint hung up and grinned at Sergio. Sergio returned the grin.

Clint went home and called Manny. Judi made a delicious lobster chowder. It was good to be home among friends.

"Well, it looks like Marko was able to get the chest to the people on that island," Clint told Nikolo, who had come to Bocas Town to visit and see the area. He said he rather liked it.

"Yes. Things are going well. Better than ever before in anyone's remembrance. The people got their first payment, a little more than four hundred thousand apiece, the medical facility is contracted and teachers are coming to staff the schools. We have another problem I should have foreseen, but it will work out, I imagine."

"What's that?"

"Nobody will show up for work. A millionaire does not find himself in the position where he must carry large and dirty items across wet and stinking docks, nor must they work in stores or banks or whatever."

Clint laughed. "We really should have seen that one coming!"

"Well, they can now give honest employment to many others in the near area. It will greatly help economies of several of the islands there. It will take a short while to get things operating correctly again. The United States has sent personnel to man the facilities to keep the port in operation with only small delay. Vendors from the small islands nearby will bring in food and supplies to sell. It will work out. People will become bored with nothing to do and will find work suitable to their psychologies."

Judi and Dave came in the front door, yelling that they were there and hungry. They came onto the deck, where Clint and Nikolo were lounging. They apologized for the rude entrance. Nikolo waved and said he was also hungry, so would treat them all to a good meal in the restaurant of their choice.

"I was making some gunk, there's plenty, so we'll take you up on that another time," Clint said. "You guys, this is Nikolo, who you've heard me mention. Dave and Judi. You can entertain each other while I do the finishing touches thing."

He went to the kitchen and took the Yankee pot roast he was fixing out of the slow cooker and put it in a large pot to finish cooking. He made a salad of various fruits, set the table, and yelled to come and get it or he'd throw it to the fish. They came in, laughing and joking. It was a great time.

That night, Nikolo took them and Ben and Earl, the gay couple in a nearby house, to dinner at the Nine Degrees. Nikolo stayed at the Tropical Suites, where Clint told the employees that King Fatuous was going to do twenty years.

Nikolo went back to Costa Rica the next day. Clint went back home to lay around a bit.

What now? Fishing? Maybe visit his friends on the comarca?

He'd think of something.

C. D. Moulton's works are available on most major outlets as printed or e-books. CD writes the CD Grimes, PI, mysteries, the Det. Lt. Nick Storie mysteries, the Clint Faraday mysteries, the Flight of the Maita science fiction series, books on orchid culture and many others of many types. Mystery, adventure, intrigue, science fiction, humor, fantasy, paranormal, mild erotica, and factual.